595

D1177633

SPACE CAT

MEETS MARS

SPACE CAT

MEETS MARS

By RUTHVEN TODD

Illustrated by
PAUL GALDONE

Charles Scribner's Sons   **New York**

For Christopher Wilbur

SPACE CAT

MEETS MARS

CHAPTER
ONE

Flyball yawned. He lay back in his specially-built hammock on board the good spaceship *Halley* and grumbled quietly to himself about the terrible dullness of space travel. Long, long ago when he had made his first journey through space, from the Earth to the Moon, it had been new and exciting. Floating around the cabin of that early rocket ship, the ZOX-1, had been fun. So had been the job of chasing drops of milk which were, like himself, in free-fall.

Now, however, he was a seasoned space cat, veteran of several Earth-Moon and Moon-Earth journeys, always in company with his constant companion, Colonel Fred Stone.

As a result of all these Moon trips, the two of them had set out in this most fancy spaceship, the *Halley*, called after the great astronomer. They had meant to go to Venus and had succeeded in getting there. Now they were on their way home, to live on Earth, where there were birds and mice.

Flyball forgot the dullness of travel and purred quietly to himself as he thought things over. Venus had been an odd place indeed, with sensible plants and only one kind of animal, a rather dumb blue creature, somewhat like a six-legged mouse.

Still, though Flyball as a rule had little use for vegetables, despising cabbage and ignoring spinach, he had to admit that the Venusian plants had been unlike those of Earth, and really clever. They had given him and Fred Stone little pieces of a moss called *pyxyx*, which, dangling in little lockets around their necks, had enabled them to read each other's thoughts.

But now, well away from the gravity of Venus, the moss had stopped working. It was a pity in a way. Yet, even though Flyball and Fred could no longer exchange their thoughts, the fact that they had once been able to do so, even for a short time, meant that they understood each other better than any man or cat had ever done before.

4

Fred knew that Flyball understood him when he talked, even if he could not answer back, and Flyball knew that Fred understood what he meant by his different behaviors.

For a first, exploratory, expedition to Venus they had done rather well. The *Halley* was carrying dozens of envelopes of seeds which were to be planted on Earth. Someday, as plants, they would be sent back to Venus so that the stay-at-home plants there would get some idea of a different world where animals, and not plants, were the intelligent life.

As well as the seeds, they were carrying many chunks of a most curious red crystal which was harder than a diamond, but which could be melted and worked with the help of the juice of a strange tree called the *tlora*. They had several gallon bottles of this juice.

Fred Stone, who was lying in his hammock, finally finished his book and closed it. He stretched and got up. He agreed with Flyball that, usually, space travel was just plain old dull. Taking-off and landing needed skill and attention, but once one had got up enough speed there was nothing to do but keep an eye on things, for the *Halley* was almost completely automatically controlled.

He started wandering round the cabin, held to the walls, floor and ceiling by magnets in the soles of his shoes. Then, he looked at all the various dials which showed how they were going along.

Suddenly he straightened up, and Flyball could tell there was something wrong.

"What on Earth, or on the Moon, can be the matter?" Fred exclaimed. "Only a few hours ago we were right on the beam and here we are wandering off it! And wandering badly!"

He scowled at the instruments, and fishing a piece of pencil out of a pocket, started to make calculations on a scratch pad.

Flyball, who couldn't do arithmetic, just had to wait until Fred spoke again. But he could tell that Fred was seriously worried.

Fred stood up and pressed a series of buttons, and all over the ship heavy metal shields slid away from thick glass portholes.

Flyball who, like all cats, did not believe in moving unless he had to when he was comfortable, looked out of the porthole nearest to him. About half a mile away, floating idly in space, he saw a great ragged chunk of rock, rather bigger than the biggest building he had ever seen.

Fred gazed out too and then grabbed a pair of binoculars. He examined the large black rock for a long moment. Then he turned again to the instruments and looked them over carefully.

Finally, he ran his fingers through his hair, looking both worried and puzzled.

"It's sheer bad luck, Flyball, and that's all there is to it," he said at last. "We've been captured by an asteroid."

He started pulling charts of the sky out of a drawer and soon they were scattered all over a

8

shelf which he slid out of the wall. The shelf had strips of steel on it and the charts had magnetized tape on their backs which prevented their flying around the cabin like bats.

"Asteroids? Asteroids, what are they?" Flyball thought crossly. He knew the word all right, but he had not really been paying much attention when the men in the big observatory on the Moon had talked about such things. He gave a yowl to attract Fred's attention and to show that he wanted information.

"Well, Flyball," said Fred, "asteroids are really nothing more than little planets. They are too small to have any atmosphere, but quite big enough to capture us in their field of gravity, I'm afraid. Of course, with our rockets, we'll be able to break free easily enough. But before I fire the rockets, I've got to do some more figuring. We don't want to be flying off to Jupiter by mistake!"

Flyball supposed that they did not, although he did not really care where he went. He could take his adventures as they came to him. Jupiter, Neptune, Mercury, Saturn, Uranus, or even the outer stars, it was all the same to him. He and Fred could go *anywhere*, just so long as they had a good spaceship!

Fred, seeing the flick of Flyball's whiskers, chuckled grimly. "We wouldn't be much good on a planet where we'd find ourselves so heavy that we could not move," he added.

Flyball raised a paw and examined it solemnly. There certainly would not be much fun on a world where he could not bounce and spring, and where no birds could fly. He yawned again and twitched his whiskers. It really was too silly worrying about things such as that. Fred would never land them in a place where they could not walk.

He lolled back in his hammock and looked at the magnetic pads he wore strapped to the pads of his paws. Wearing these sticky things was bad enough without trying to imagine places where he could not even walk. He closed his eyes and thought of mice.

It seemed a long time later that Fred straightened up and looked at the spaceship's special clock. He pressed the buttons that closed the shields over the portholes and moved over to Flyball's hammock, where he started strapping him in.

"I'm going to have to fire the rockets," he explained, "so we'll have to be strapped in. I think we should put on our space suits too."

11

Flyball bristled. He did not like having to wear his suit, and he considered the helmet a globe suitable only for silly goldfish.

Fred seemed to change his mind. He went over to his own hammock and fastened himself in, with the firing buttons under his right hand.

"Ready, Flyball," he called and then, watching the clock as he did so, he pressed the buttons. For a moment there was a tremendous roar and both he and Flyball were flattened in their hammocks.

Suddenly the roar was cut in halves. As the pressure lessened, Flyball was able to twist his head and look across at his friend.

The knuckles of Fred's hand were white as he pressed, and pressed again, on the buttons that fired the starboard rockets. But there was no answering roar. He jabbed a bar and, as quickly as it had begun, the noise stopped and there was no more pressure.

"Something wrong on the starboard side," Fred said, trying to sound cheerful, although he knew that he could not hide his worry from Flyball. He unstrapped himself and then did the same for Flyball, who rolled out of his hammock. Being weightless, he could not jump as he would have done on Earth.

Fred slid back the porthole covers and looked out.

"Well," he remarked, "at least we've shaken off our asteroid. But now I've got to discover just where we are headed for."

Flyball wished, just for a moment, that he could exchange thoughts with Fred once again.

"Who knows," he pondered, "but that as a cat, and a very clever cat at that, I might not be able to make helpful suggestions."

There was nothing he could do about it, however. Fred was busy taking sights with all sorts of instruments, making notes and shaking his head. Flyball wished he would not worry so by himself.

"Well, Flyball," he said in a funny voice, as he sat down on the edge of his hammock, "we're completely off our orbit. We'll need to think what we can do next. At the moment, it doesn't look as though we've got the least hope of making our base on the Moon. All I can do is see whether, with a burst of the port rockets, we can make for Mars. If we could land there I might be able to do the necessary repairs. Maybe, if we give them a rest, the starboard rockets will fire enough to enable us to land."

Once more they strapped themselves into their hammocks and Fred, studying a piece of paper covered with calculations, gave a series of short bursts on the port rockets.

"That should do it," he said at length.

CHAPTER
TWO

Ahead of them the glaring red sphere which was Mars grew steadily bigger and bigger. Flyball, glad that they were not lost in space, no longer grumbled to himself about the dullness of space travel. It was good to be inside the nice, comfortable cabin, warm, with plenty to eat. And bound for a definite place.

As the days went by, he noticed Fred glancing at him. He wondered what was the matter, but the glances were amused and not worried. Then, one day, when he was eating his food from the funny plastic bag which kept it from escaping into the cabin, Fred spoke.

"You're not getting enough exercise," he said.

"And you *are* eating a lot. If you're not careful, you'll find yourself getting fat."

"Who? Fat? Me?" Flyball thought most indignantly. All the same, when he knew Fred was not watching him, he ran a stealthy paw over his sleek tummy. He was very thoughtful, for he was sure he could just feel a bulge which had not been there when they left the Moon for the flight to Venus.

This was worse than a pretty kettle of fish, he thought. As a space cat he could not let himself get fat. Why, if that happened, he might find that he could no longer fit in his space suit. Much as he loathed it, that would never do!

So, for the rest of the journey, he took to tumbling around the cabin, this way and that, in the hope that the exercise, though not as healthy as mouse-chasing, would lessen the bulge. And he was terribly careful about what, and how much, he ate. He was, he told himself, Space Cat and not Fat Cat!

As they drew nearer and nearer to the red planet, Flyball wondered what they would find there. Both the Moon and Venus had, in their different ways, been somewhat of disappointments to him. He had hoped that somewhere in space he would find mice and birds. But when he

16

had run into something rather like a mouse on Venus, he had discovered that he was not allowed to chase it!

Now Mars, he purred hopefully, twiddling his whiskers, might be different. Surely it might have mice for him! He had been in space for so long, chasing around after planets, that he had almost forgotten what it was like to chase a mouse!

At last they were close enough to look at Mars, as it filled the whole of the portholes which looked out ahead. Fred sat making even more calculations.

"It would never do," he said at last, "for us to get as far as this and then crash the ship into one of the little moons of Mars. Besides, we want, if we can, to land on one of the green patches you can see. If we were to land in the red deserts, we might run into dust storms which make those of Texas and Oklahoma feel like sea breezes. So we want to try one of the green places."

"Bah, more vegetables," thought Flyball, rather rudely.

Now that they were closer they could see that the green patches were broken with smears and spots of red, yellow, black, gray and brown. Through this colored area there ran the deeper

18

green of the canals, streaking the landscape toward the deserts which were the color of powdered brick.

As they approached the scudding clouds, they once more got into their hammocks. When Fred pressed the buttons that were supposed to fire the rockets, they both held their breaths. They wondered whether he had been right in guessing that, after a rest, the starboard rockets might fire long enough to land them.

There was a moment's pause and then they were flattened in their hammocks and pulled around as the *Halley* turned her tail toward the surface of Mars. The rockets were firing all right, on both sides.

Just a few feet from the ground, Fred struck the bar and lifted his hand as if he had finished playing a piece of music. The ship dropped suddenly and then, with a slight jar, came to rest. In spite of everything they had made a perfect landing.

Fred opened the portholes and they looked out at a most curious landscape. All around them were lichens, but not lichens such as grew on Earth— little crusts on rocks or small straggly beards on trees. Here the lichens, milky green and mottled with other colors, were enormous curled and

19

rolled shapes and thick, long, tangled strands. Among the lichens grew fungi of all sorts and shapes and sizes. Mushrooms as big and bigger than truck wheels grew beside vast puffballs; great trumpet-shapes raised their purple vases around them; and, on ledges, there were enormous shelf-fungi which would have served as dining tables for a banquet.

Flyball, impatient as always, went to the air lock and miaowed. He wanted to get out. After all, he told himself, where there were plants there was bound to be air, which would let him breathe.

Fred, however, took out their space suits and made Flyball get into his. Then they went into the air lock and at long last were once more able to stand on the ground.

Cooped up in his space suit Flyball had to wait patiently while Fred made a series of experiments. As he did so his face took on a puzzled look. He tried the air at different heights from the ground and, finally, his expression cleared.

"You'll be better off than I will, Flyball," he told his friend. "The oxygen here is given off by the plants. As you are nearer the ground than I am, you'll get more of it. Mmm," he looked thoughtful, "that means we'll have to get into the ship for the nights and use our own air. Plants only make oxygen during the hours of daylight. During the nights they give off carbon dioxide and we can't breathe that!"

Flyball was not paying much attention to this scientific explanation. Now that he knew that he could breathe on Mars, he was only waiting to be released from his space suit, to run and bound around.

Once out of the suit, Flyball found that he could indeed run freely. When he jumped into the air, he did not come down with a bump. While he did not float as gently as on the Moon, his fall was still slow-motion. He looked at Fred and yowled for an explanation.

"Oh, you're only about a third of your Earth weight here," Fred told him. "Say you were eight Earth pounds when we left the Moon, we'd better call you ten pounds now to allow for the weight you've put on during the journey." Flyball glowered at him furiously. "That'll make you weigh around three and a half pounds here. Now, I'll go take a look at these tubes and see what's been making them play up."

Flyball, very much on his dignity, stalked off among the lichens and mushrooms, his fine bushy

21

tail standing up like a flagpole. He was certain that he had not put on all that weight during the voyage. All the same, he had to admit that it was difficult to tell when he had felt so delightfully light. It was just the right kind of lightness after the weightlessness of free-fall.

As he went, he wondered whether the Martian plants had any sense, and bumped against them rudely. But they showed no more feeling than a cauliflower would have done on Earth.

When he patted a long tendril of lichen out of his way, something, about the size of a sparrow, rose in the air and fluttered round him. Sitting up on his haunches, Flyball batted at it. It really was flying too close to him. In fact, it was almost getting in his whiskers, a thing no bird on Earth would have done.

He caught it a glancing blow, and obediently it came to the ground in front of him. There it sat, looking at him gravely out of big staring blue eyes which, instead of being round and smooth as his own, were many-faced, like crystals.

He stared back at the creature, which had four legs and sat up on the long back pair. He knew he had seen something rather like it before. He sat down more comfortably and examined it thought-

fully, combing his whiskers as he did so. The thing —for it certainly was not a bird, if he knew birds as he was sure he did—did not appear to be the least bit frightened.

Even when Flyball pushed out a paw and prodded it, it did not fly away. There was no fun in birds, or whatever this thing was, which would not fly away when he threatened them. An Earth bird would have perched just out of reach and mocked at him, until he jumped at it, only to find it being impudent from another place.

He went on glaring at the thing, trying to recall what it was that it looked like. At last he had it. It was really something like a grasshopper, though much bigger and with fewer legs.

"Bah!" said Flyball to himself. "I'm not a kitten any more, to go chasing after grasshoppers—even Martian ones!"

He rose and moved to one side to pass the thing. But, pop, there it stood in front of him again. Try as he would to pass it, the thing jumped in front of him. It was examining him, too, he suddenly realized, and it had not got through with its inspection as quickly as he had. He felt just a little put-out at being stared at by an insect.

Sitting down again, he tried to outstare the

thing, but that was not easy, for while he had only two eyes, it seemed to have thousands fitted into the space where it should have had two. At last, however, it seemed to have finished. It dropped one lemon yellow eyelid in a kind of wink and took off with a dry flutter of its hard wings. It buzzed round Flyball's head a couple of times and then flew away.

Flyball lay for a moment, purring quietly to himself. If there were things like grasshoppers, there might well be birds on Mars. He started back toward the ship, forgetting that he had left with his tail up. He wanted to see how Fred was getting on.

Back at the *Halley* he found a great ring of the grasshopper things gathered round the ship watching Fred, who was wearing overalls, working away with a hammer and a cold chisel.

Flyball took a leap right over the spectators, which did not disturb them in the least, and strolled toward his friend.

Fred looked up and smiled.

"Good to see you, pal," he said. "I wish, however, that our friends here could lend me a hand instead of just sitting and staring. It makes me nervous."

Flyball twitched a whisker in agreement, and looked down at the ground which was covered with bright clear blue chips, like broken glass.

26

"Oh, yes," Fred went on, "I've found the trouble. The tubes are almost closed with the blue sand of Venus, which must have fused under the heat of our take-off. The stuff is terribly hard and I want to get the tubes absolutely clear before we leave. We don't want to risk their clogging up out in space again."

Flyball whisked his fine sleek tail, showing that he agreed.

The grasshopper things went on watching them, without showing much real curiosity. It made Flyball feel funny to be watched by so many millions of eyes. A cat, he had heard, could look at a king, but nobody had ever said that grasshoppers could look at a cat. He decided that he had to escape from the inspection. There was nothing he could do to help Fred. He could not swing a sledge-hammer or wield a cold chisel.

He turned away. Fred looked up at the sun which, although Mars is farther away from it than the Earth, looked just as big, if not bigger, because of the thin atmosphere.

"Be sure to get back before the sun sets, Flyball," he warned. "It isn't very warm now, and after dark it will become horribly cold—colder than any place on Earth."

Flyball pounced over the grasshoppers and jumped up on top of a huge mushroom. He paused there to wash his face, and looked at Fred working on the tubes, watched by all those strange eyes.

He glanced around him, with the mildly bored air of an experienced space cat. Away to one side he could see the dark green gutter of one of the Martian canals.

CHAPTER THREE

His sleek tail waving gently on high, Flyball went in search of adventure. He picked his way carefully round vast crumpled lichens, with thick, many-branched trunks topped with scarlet caps. Every now and again he would jump up on one of the giant mushrooms, or climb the enormous steps of a shelf-fungus, to check that he was going in the right direction.

When he did this, he realized that Fred had not been talking nonsense. When he was perched high upon one of these fungi, he noticed how thin the air was. It was as thin as it might have been flying five miles up, or on top of Mount Everest on Earth. That would explain why Fred had looked a little tired while he, Flyball, felt as fresh and frisky as a kitten.

30

The sun was well past its peak and Flyball kept one wary eye upon it. He had no wish to be turned into a deep-frozen space cat, as would happen if he stayed out for the night, for the temperature of Mars would get down to about a hundred and fifty degrees below freezing.

Crawling on a slowly rotting mushroom was a most beautiful creature. It was rather like a ladybug on Earth, but was nearly as big as Flyball. It was a brilliant green with bright orange spots, as big as oranges.

Flyball arched his back and put his bristling tail straight up, strong and erect as an iron fence post. His whiskers stood out straight and quivered. The ladybug looked at him solemnly out of deep brown eyes. Flyball bared his sharp teeth, and flexed his claws in their sheaths. The ladybug did not seem in the least frightened. Flyball put out a paw and slapped it gently. The ladybug did not mind a bit. He gave it a little push, but it would not budge an inch.

Then it looked down at the fungus again and paid no more attention to Flyball.

He was a little disgusted. What was the use of creatures that would not even play, and that did not seem interested in the things they saw?

He went on his way, quietly ignored by the ladybug, who really was more interested in the mushroom.

On Earth, Flyball thought, insects were of a decent size and even a self-respecting cat could occasionally get a little fun out of them, pretending to jump like a grasshopper, or sitting on a window sill swatting flies on the pane. But here they were too big and did not even try to run away from him. It really was too bad. After being shut up in a spaceship for all that time, and after the plant life of Venus, he really might have expected some fun with the creatures on Mars.

He plodded on toward the canal, feeling just a little depressed. Then he cheered up. At least, while Fred was busy working on the tubes, *he* could do the exploring for the expedition. His steps became brisker.

He was an explorer now, a fully qualified space cat, and no longer a kitten, to fritter away his time chasing insignificant insects.

"Poo on all insects," he thought. Now birds— ah, birds, these were a different matter! They were warm-blooded, as he himself was warm-blooded, and not cold as snakes and crabs. He had to admit to himself that crab, removed from its horny shell,

made a very acceptable meal, but live crabs were cold as insects. But, most of all, there were these wonderful creatures called mice! He sighed as he thought longingly of mice.

As if the very thought of mice had suddenly called one into being, he was shocked to see a mouse just ahead of him. Its back was turned toward him and it did not see him, but he was too experienced a mouser to be mistaken. He flattened himself on the ground, hidden by a crinkled fold of lichen, and examined the mouse doubtfully.

At least it *looked* like a mouse, for the ears and tail were in the right places. But, where an Earth mouse was furry, this one was as shiny as if it had been chromium-plated. The lichens and mushrooms were reflected in its bright skin.

Flyball began squirming his way toward it, keeping hidden under the furled and cockled lichens.

The mouse paid no attention. It was busy licking up the sweet juice that was trickling down the stem of a mushroom.

Flyball wriggled a little closer to the shining mouse and gathered himself for a spring. Then he snarled softly. It would not be fair to pounce on a mouse when its back was turned.

34

The mouse put its head round and looked at him out of gleaming ruby eyes. When it had taken in Flyball, its gleaming round ears perked up. Then it darted a little to one side, but Flyball, with an easy spring, was there in front of it.

The mouse ran the other way, but again, helped by the fact that he could jump two and a half times as far as on Earth, Flyball was there first.

"Ah, ha," said Flyball, softly to himself. "This is the life! Mice at last! I *knew* we'd catch up with them sooner or later!"

The mouse ran this way and that, but Flyball, taking tremendous leaps, was always ahead of it. He was enjoying himself. This was the sort of exercise he needed to take away that faint suggestion of a bulge on his tummy, which just might have developed during the voyage.

At last, the mouse sat still between his paws. Flyball was not ready to give up yet. He gave it a soft pat, to start it running again, and got the surprise of his life. Instead of being soft, as he had expected in spite of its glittering skin, the mouse was just as hard as the outside of the spaceship, and that was very hard indeed.

Flyball put his mouth gently to it, but the mouse made no attempt to run away. He picked it up tenderly, as he would have done with a mouse on Earth. Not only was it hard—it was heavy too. He held it for a moment, till he thought the weight would damage his needle-sharp teeth. Then he laid it down again.

The mouse looked at him for a moment with round eyes and then it made a run. Flyball realized that instead of *his* playing with the mouse, *it* was playing with him. Very well, if that was the way it wanted it, he would go along. He could play too.

He had to admit that even if he could not bite it and his swats made no impression, this hard, heavy mouse gave him as much sport as any soft, furry, lightweight mouse had ever done on Earth. In fact, it was much cleverer than any Earth mouse. It dodged much better and it sometimes seemed to be on the point of escaping him altogether, though it always came back for more. It would run behind a feathery lichen and peer out at him and then, quick as a streak, it would be somewhere else entirely.

It did not seem to be the least frightened of him, but would often jump between his paws, cock its head and look up at him in a cheeky manner. Flyball would bat it and it would roll away, head-over-heels, and still it would come back toward him. It took Flyball all his time to keep up with its tricks, and he was convinced that no ordinary Earth cat could have managed as well as he did. He certainly had plenty of exercise.

At last, however, the armor-plated mouse, as Flyball thought of it, got tired of the game. It returned to its leaking fungus and went on supping up the sweet juice that dribbled down the stalk.

Nothing that Flyball could do would make it go on playing. He rolled it over once or twice and it did not seem the least frightened or annoyed. It just picked itself up and went on eating. As far as it was concerned, the game was over. At least for the time being.

Feeling ever so much better, Flyball jumped up on top of a big red mushroom, dotted with rough whitish warts which helped him clamber up to the umbrella-shaped peak. He looked back at the *Halley*. Fred was still working away at the rocket tubes. Then Flyball glanced at the sun. There was still time for him to get to the canal and back before it got too cold, if he did not dawdle with mice on the way.

His tail once more stuck in the air like a private flag. Flyball, ignoring peculiar insects, made his way toward the dark green streak which stood out so clearly against the more milky green of the lichens. It was, Flyball reminded himself, quite a time since he had seen plain old water. There was none on the Moon, and on Venus it had all tasted of ammonia. So there had been no fish and Flyball liked fish, particularly fresh fish. He was getting just a little tired of fish out of cans. Perhaps, once he had the rocket tubes fixed, Fred would go fishing!

Along the banks of the canal, when he finally reached it, Flyball found that the lichens gave way to other plants. There were enormous-leaved vegetables, like vast rhubarb plants, and among them grew giant vines, bearing many-colored pea-like flowers.

Flyball had to push his way through this vegetation as it did not, obligingly, get out of his way as the thinking plants on Venus had done. Though in some ways these plants were somewhat like Earth plants, they could never have been mistaken for them. But when Flyball reached the very edge of the canal, he found that that, at least, was ordinary water.

Flyball sat and gazed into the still water, not moving at all, though he rather admired the reflection of his handsome face and would have liked to groom his elegant whiskers.

He sat as still as a statue, and several times he thought he saw something moving in the water. But it was not until the sun was sending long slanting rays across the unrippled surface that his patience was properly rewarded and he caught sight of his first Martian fish. It was long and thin and pale gold in color.

It swam up toward him unafraid, pouting its mouth toward the surface, almost as if it wanted to speak to him. He wiggled his whiskers at it and it blew a bubble back at him.

Flyball had never had a fish blow bubbles at him before, so he stood up and arched his back and hissed at it. The fish paid no attention but merely blew another bubble.

At that moment there was a splash on the other side of the canal, and a ring of ripples spread rapidly across it. Flyball, occupied with his fish, was a moment late in looking up, but he caught a glimpse of a red figure sliding away among the rhubarb plants.

Of course it could not be what it looked like. A red cat, a fire-engine red cat!

"Miaow!" said Flyball loudly. If it was a cat it surely would understand that. He looked hard but there was no sign of the figure he thought he had seen.

Flyball tickled his ear thoughtfully. He could not really believe that he had seen a *cat*. He must have been imagining things in the failing light of the sun.

"The failing light of the sun!" He repeated his thought. The sun was almost down and he remembered what Fred had said. "Be sure to get back before the sun sets, Flyball."

Without stopping to make a good-bye face at the fish, which was still blowing bubbles, he turned and, after pushing his way through the thick plants, bounded off in the direction of the *Halley*. The only pause he made was once when he pranced up the steps of a giant shelf-fungus to see that he was still going the right way.

He had no time to think. All he wanted to do was to get to the ship before the sun set, taking with it the oxygen which he needed to breathe. Besides, he had no wish to become a frozen space cat.

Already it was getting cold. He had been so occupied at the side of the canal that he had not noticed it. He bounded and swerved over and around the lichen and fungi which grew between him and the ship.

As he ran, he noticed a difference in the quality of the air his lungs were getting. But as he was travelling as fast as he could, and had not run so hard for a long time, it was difficult to say whether it was a change in the atmosphere or merely short-ness of breath after all that exercise!

He was pretty exhausted when, rounding the edge of a lichen, he saw the *Halley* just ahead of him. Fred was standing at the top of the steps, in the door of the air lock, with his binoculars in his hands, raising them for another sweep around the wrinkled landscape.

"Where have you been, Flyball?" he asked anx-iously, as his friend bounded up the steps to join him. "I was beginning to be afraid you'd be caught by the night—and I didn't know where to find you."

Flyball, recovering his breath, tilted his head in the direction of the canal. He wished he could tell Fred about his adventures of the afternoon, about the other insects, the mouse and the fish. But not about the cat. He still was not sure about that.

Safely inside the ship, Fred opened the special deep-space refrigerator and took out a can.

Flyball had not realized how hungry he was. Even with the memory of that fine fresh golden fish still in his mind, he found his platter of tuna most pleasing. But he did not eat too much, as he did not want to undo all the good that might have been done during his chase of the armored mouse and his mad dash for the ship.

CHAPTER
FOUR

With the glaring sun shining down on them, although not nearly as hotly as it would have done on Earth, Fred and Flyball ate their breakfast at one of the great shelf-fungi outside the *Halley*. Flyball, of course, ate on top of the one that served as table, but there was a smaller shelf at just the right height to make a chair for Fred.

"Well," said Fred, after he had cleared up. "I've still got a lot of work ahead of me." He struggled into his overalls and picked up his tools—hammers, chisels and scrapers. "You might as well see what you can, but don't get into trouble."

Flyball flicked his head. *He* never got into trouble. It was only human beings who got into trouble.

Leaving Fred chipping away at the tubes, he set off once more in the direction of the canal. He only stopped once on the way and that was to give one of the hard, heavy mice a friendly knocking about. This time the mouse would have gone on with the game for a longer time, but Flyball remembered his errand. He bustled on toward the canal.

He worked his way through the elephant-eared rhubarb plants and the elephant trunks of the vines, and took up his position near where he had sat the day before.

Soon there were no less than seven of the adoring golden fish, gazing up at him with light green eyes, blowing bubbles to attract his attention. They seemed to expect something from him, but he had no idea of what it could be.

However, Flyball did not pay much attention to the fish. He was watching the other bank of the canal.

"No," he said to himself, "you won't see anything. You were just imagining things last night.

It was the fading light and the oxygen going down."

One of the fish blew a bubble which burst with an especially loud plop! Flyball looked down, and when he looked up again—there it stood on the far side!

A really red, a really fire-engine red, cat! It stood there, gazing across at him.

This cat was about his own size, but where his stripes ran down his body, the few stripes the red cat had, of a slightly darker red, ran from its head toward its narrowly ringed tail.

"Miaow," said Flyball, softly. He did not want to frighten it away. As he spoke, he was suddenly aware that although he might sometimes be awfully snooty about cats who were not space cats, it really was a long time since he had had a good long talk with one of his own kind.

"Meeowee!" answered the Martian cat, rather louder, with its pink whiskers shivering.

Flyball nearly fell into the canal in surprise. He knew what the Martian cat was saying! Its accent was different from that of the cats he had known on Earth, but it still was speaking perfectly good Cat. It wanted to know where he came from and who he was.

47

"How do you do?" Flyball was polite. "My name is Flyball and I come from Earth." He waved a paw grandly at the sky as he was not sure in which direction Earth lay.

"My name is Moofa," the other replied. "Why don't you come over for a chat?"

"Come over?" Flyball asked, looking at all that wet water. "How?"

"Swim, silly," Moofa was not too polite. Flyball looked at the water again and shuddered, right down to the ends of his whiskers. He was not at all fond of getting wet. "Oh, well, if you can't," Moofa went on, "I must."

Without hesitation she plunged into the water. Although Flyball had heard that cats *could* swim, he had never seen one actually do so. With pop-eyes he watched Moofa as, with easy strokes, she swam toward him. It certainly did not look very difficult, but at the same time he was glad he was not in the water with Moofa. It was not only wet, but also cold.

Moofa scrambled up on the bank beside him. Giving herself a shake which sent drops of water flying from the pink tips of her whiskers, she cast a long look at Flyball.

"My, what a beautiful color you are," she said at last.

Flyball, who knew he was a most handsome gray cat, was not to be outdone.

"I was just about to say the same of you," he replied. They stood for a moment, admiring one another.

"How would you like a fish?" asked Moofa, changing the subject. She was looking down at the

50

golden fish which, seeing *two* cats, were now blowing bubbles more merrily than ever.

"Very much indeed," said Flyball politely. "How do you catch them though?"

"You'll see," answered Moofa, with just a touch of superiority in her tone. It suggested that a cat who did not know how to fish was no cat at all.

She pushed her way through the thick plants and reappeared a moment later carrying a slab of spongy fungus in her mouth. She laid this down and broke it up into fragments with her fore paws.

The fish leaped in the water with excitement.

Moofa shovelled the crumbled fungus off the bank and the fish crowded round it eagerly.

She examined the bustling fish with an experienced eye and then, leaning over the water, hooked out the fattest one with an expert paw and killed it with a quick thump behind the head.

"How's that?" she asked, with just a suggestion of pride in her voice.

Flyball, being a clever cat himself and admiring cleverness in others, was most enthusiastic.

"I don't know how you do it," he said, and he really meant it.

He could never have caught a fish in an open canal, himself. The nearest he had ever got to fishing was trying to flip a goldfish out of a bowl, and then his paws had got too wet and that had discouraged him.

"Oh, it's nothing, really," replied Moofa, looking modest, as she neatly divided the fish between them. "I was brought up to do it as a kitten. And if you learn young enough, anything is easy!"

"Are there many cats on Mars?" Flyball wanted to know. This was a superior cat. A cat in his own class. Though he really liked his fish cooked, he made a start on the portion that Moofa pushed toward him and had to admit that it was good.

"So far as I know," Moofa replied, curling her tongue to pick a piece of fish from her whiskers, "I'm the last. When I'm gone there will be *no* cats on Mars!"

"I never expected to meet an ordinary—oh, I'm sorry—I mean a cat the same as myself here," Flyball said. He thought he detected a note of sorrow in Moofa's voice and did not want to press the subject.

"Oh, cats are *everywhere*." Moofa was positive. Flyball thought for a moment and realized that what she said was nearly true. Cats, he had heard from Fred during their long voyages, were holy animals in ancient Egypt and were made into

52

mummies just like human kings and queens. Now that he thought of it, there was no reason why there should *not* be cats on Mars, for there certainly were mice, even if they were odd mice. Moofa, on the other hand, seemed to be odd only in her coloring and—in her fishing and swimming habits.

She looked up at the sky, at the scurrying clouds. She twitched her red ears as if listening to something that Flyball could not hear.

"Storm coming up fast," she announced at last. "We'd better get under cover."

"Wow!" said Flyball. "I must get back to the ship. Fred's there and he'll be worried. These humans." Moofa looked puzzled, not knowing what a human was. "These humans do worry so!" added Flyball.

"Where's your ship?" asked Moofa, wiping the last of the fish off her whiskers.

Flyball led the way through the thick plants and they both jumped up on top of a pale lavender mushroom.

"There." Flyball waved a paw toward it.

Moofa glanced up at the sky again and at the distant *Halley*. She scratched her nose thoughtfully.

"I don't think you can make it," she said. "I know a place near here. We'd better go there."

"No!" Flyball was firm. "I've got to go to Fred. He won't know what to do without me."

He jumped off the mushroom and started loping along as fast as he could. Suddenly he was aware that Moofa was running beside him.

"You don't need to come," he edged out between his thinned mouth.

"Of course, I do." Moofa answered, "You wouldn't know what to do if you were caught in the storm."

Already the sky was darkening and the wind was pushing hard behind them, whipping them with brick-colored grains of sand. They ran as fast as they could, but Flyball had a sneaking feeling that if he had not been with her, Moofa could have run even faster.

It grew darker and darker and the wind blew harder and harder. The specks of red dust stung like thousands of bees, and still the *Halley* was a long way off.

Then, in front of them in the murk, they saw a strange figure coming toward them, bent almost double as it fought against the wind.

Flyball jumped up on it. It was Fred, his calls for Flyball being carried away behind him.

Fred did not speak. He could not, for he was covered from head to foot with the thick red dust. He turned, Flyball in his arms, and started to struggle back toward the *Halley*, which they could not see in the thick dust.

Then Flyball became aware that Moofa was calling loudly. "You won't make it," she cried. "You'd better follow me."

Flyball squirmed out of Fred's arms and landed on the ground. He was immediately blown over by the howling wind. He stood up and started to follow Moofa who went ahead as slowly as she could,

with the wind blasting behind her. Fred, looking through dust-filled eyes, followed them.

Suddenly Moofa rounded a bluff and there, sheltered from the wind, was a great hole in a bank. She dived into this and Flyball followed her. Fred, not seeing what else he could do, came behind. It was so dark in the cave that only cats could see clearly.

Fred slumped to the ground, and in the dark did his best to remove the grit and grime from around his mouth, nostrils and eyes. Flyball and Moofa also cleaned themselves.

When his eyes had become accustomed to the dark, Flyball was surprised to find that, in addition to Moofa, Fred and himself, the cave was also giving shelter to an enormous number of different insects and several dozen mice. He looked at the mice in astonishment, and then at Moofa, who was washing her ears with her paws.

"Oh, these," she exclaimed, giving a mouse a friendly cuff that sent it bowling across the cave. "They *do* like to play, don't they?" And the mouse ran toward her again.

The cave, dark as it had been, was growing darker. Down the funnel of the mouth there came the weird whistling of the tremendous wind. Flyball was glad he was inside, but he wondered how

Fred felt, as he knew that *he* could not see in the dark.

He jumped up on Fred's lap and lay there. Fred put a hand on his ears and pulled them back and Flyball gave a friendly purr.

The wind whistled and screamed. Even inside the cave the air became thick with choking red dust. Flyball and Fred, unused to it, kept on sneez-ing, but neither Moofa nor the others seemed the least affected by it.

Calling Moofa nearer to him, Flyball started to ask her about her life.

She was the youngest of a large family of Martian cats, the last family of cats alive on the planet. She had been left at home on the day that the rest of them had gone on an excursion into the desert. A terrible storm had sprung up suddenly and none of them had ever been seen again. Moofa had hunted and hunted for them, but with no success.

Fortunately, before her family had disappeared, they had started teaching her the art of fishing, for all Martian cats had lived by fishing as far back as their remembered history went. So she had been able to live very well, even if she often felt horribly lonely. She had cheered herself up with the thought that, perhaps, her family had been wrong, and that somewhere on Mars there might be another family of cats.

Only recently, however, having done her best to explore the whole planet, she had sadly decided that she was, indeed, the last of the Martian cats. When she had gone, there would be no more beautiful bright red cats to feed the fish and catch them.

Flyball felt terribly sorry for her. Even the armored mice could not make up for the lack of her own kind.

He changed the subject. He wanted to know how the animals managed to live through the nights.

Moofa explained that when the plants stopped giving out oxygen and during dust storms, all the Martian animals lived in the caves, which gathered oxygen enough to keep them over night, even if they could not keep out all the dust.

As she spoke, Flyball looked at her gravely in the deep gloom. Except for her beautiful bright red color, she might very well have been an Earth cat. He tried to explain to her about human beings, and how they existed only to do things for cats, even though they might think they were doing them for themselves. But Moofa could not understand, and Flyball saw that she would have to meet Fred properly once they got out of the cave. Then, perhaps, he could explain things to her.

As he thought of getting out of the cave, he jumped off Fred's lap. Fred seemed to be dozing in the dark, and so he did not feel him go. Flyball strolled toward the entrance, accompanied by Moofa.

Outside, the sky seemed to be just a little lighter, though the wind still howled as loudly. He looked inquiringly at her.

"We'll be able to go out again in a little while," she said comfortingly, "and then you'll be able to introduce me to your poor friend. It must be terrible not to be able to see in the dark. I'm not surprised that he needs you to look after him."

Flyball was getting impatient. He wanted to get out again and to show off his new friend to Fred.

"These storms die down as quickly as they spring up," said Moofa, curling her paws comfortably under her chin. "There's nothing to do but wait them out."

It seemed as though it was a long time before Moofa uncurled herself and strolled toward the entrance.

"We can go now," she announced. "There's still a lot of dust in the air, but it shouldn't worry you too much. It doesn't worry *me*."

Flyball went over and gnawed gently on Fred's hand. He woke with a start and then seemed to realize that it was all right and that it was only his friend waking him. The opening of the cave was a bright light against the dark inside and, very cautiously, he stumbled toward it.

Outside, he stood straight and sneezed and then wiped his eyes. He looked down at Flyball, then stepped back in surprise. For, instead of the one cat he had expected, there were two of them, and the new one was so beautiful that he could hardly believe his eyes.

Moofa advanced and following Flyball's example, rubbed herself against Fred's leg, sending clouds of dust into the air. She allowed him to bend down and scratch her under the chin and then pull her ears back and run his gritty hand along her back. Finally, she gave a contented purr.

She turned to Flyball. "I *like* your human being," she announced.

After a minute they turned toward the *Halley*. Already a cool fresh breeze, very different from the wind of the dust storm, was blowing the lichens and fungi clean. Fred went into the *Halley* and picked up a change of clothes.

"Before long," he told Flyball, "I'm going down to your canal and I'm going to take a swim. I'll have to do something to get this dust out of my pores."

Flyball purred approvingly. When he told Moofa what Fred had said, for, though she spoke cat language, she had never heard a human before, she also purred, and started off toward the canal.

Fred followed them, and on the bank of the canal, stripped and dived in. When he came up, he was astonished to see Moofa swimming around beside him. Flyball sat on the bank looking most disapproving. It really was tiresome of Moofa to show off like that.

"Hi, Flyball," Fred called, pushing his wet hair back. "If your friend here can swim, why can't you? Afraid of the water?"

Flyball squinted down his nose. He was not afraid of the water. It was only that he did not like the stuff. It was mean of Fred to jeer at him.

Then Moofa joined in. "Why don't you try it?" she called. "It's not difficult, and it's great fun."

Flyball glowered at both of them. Then he decided that, as a space cat, he had dared everything else, so why not even horrible, cold water?

He rose and jumped into the water with a tremendous splash, terribly different from the neat dives made by Moofa and Fred. It was, he found,

as he came up spluttering, even worse than he had expected. Not only was it cold and wet, but it got in his nose and eyes. However, he was astonished to discover that although his swimming was not as neat as Moofa's, he could keep afloat. He paddled over to the far bank and back again. Then he decided that he had shown them that he too could swim—and scrambled out.

While Moofa and Fred swam about, dodging one another and diving under, Flyball devoted his time to the job of getting all the horrible natural water out of his fur. Now that he had shown them that he, too, could swim if he wanted to do so, he was determined that he would never swim again unless he *had* to!

At last, however, both Fred and Moofa seemed to have had enough. They came to the bank and clambered out. While Fred was drying himself and dressing, Moofa came over to Flyball.

"I'm sorry," she said humbly. "I didn't mean to make you swim if you didn't want to."

"Oh, that's all right," Flyball replied, his anger disappearing. "I just wanted to show you that I could swim if I wanted to." It was, he thought, impossible to be angry with the only other cat he had encountered in space.

When Fred was dressed, they all went back toward the ship. Moofa and Flyball, the red and the grey, walked in front, with their tails stuck proudly in the air.

Moofa entered the *Halley* with them, and looked around her approvingly.

"You've got a nice place here," she said to Flyball. She was thinking of the hard life she had led on Mars, sleeping in caves which only held just enough oxygen to last the night, and fishing for food. She was delighted when Fred opened a can of sardines for her.

She ate them daintily, and licked the last luscious drop of oil from her pink whiskers. She told Flyball that she had never had a more delightful meal in all her life, and that, as a matter of cold fact, she was really getting more than a little tired of the eternal sameness of the Martian fish. They always tasted the same, day in and day out. Even when Flyball told her about it, she could not imagine the varied richness of Earth food—shrimps, cod-head, kippers, oysters and so on, and even cans of food which were specially packed for cats.

She could not quite believe in a world where cats did not have to go out to fish for their own fish, but kept people to do the job for them.

Until the storm had blown up so suddenly, Fred had been making good progress with his job of clearing the rocket-tubes. He had found out that rather than chip away the blue glass with a cold chisel, he could flake it off in larger pieces by banging the outsides of the tubes.

While he went on with his work, Flyball and Moofa went for another walk in the cool of the afternoon sun, with the soft breeze blowing away the last of the dust.

While they examined all the strange mushrooms which she showed him, Flyball told Moofa more about life on Earth and his own life as a space cat. She was most interested.

Finally, when they were once more sitting by the side of the canal, paying no attention to the bubbling of the fish, Flyball looked straight at her.

"Won't you feel awfully lonely once we go off again?" he asked, twiddling his whiskers delicately with his paw. Moofa put her head thoughtfully on a ruby-colored pad and gazed into the water.

"Yes, I suppose I shall," she admitted. "It'll be worse than it was before you came. Until I caught a glimpse of you yesterday, I thought I was perhaps the only cat in the universe."

"That's just what I meant," Flyball went on, combing out his whiskers with shining white claws. "I don't know how you'd like it, but there is room for you on the *Halley*. Would you like to come with us?"

Moofa watched the fish for a moment before she spoke. "It'll be very strange," she said slowly, "but there's really no point in going on being the last cat on Mars, now that I know about you others. The fish will get by without me. Yes, I'll come with you—if your Fred will let me."

"Of course he will," replied Flyball, showing more conviction in his voice than he really felt.

As they drew near to the ship, they noticed that Fred was no longer whanging away at the tubes. He was seated on the ground, sewing away like mad.

"Miaow," said Flyball gently, and Fred looked up. It was too late for him to hide his work. Flyball could see it was a cat-sized hammock.

"Well," said Fred, "you surprised me too soon. I'd hoped to have this fitted up for your friend by the time you got back. I suppose you want to take her with us?"

For answer, both Flyball and Moofa rubbed against his legs, purring loudly.

Late that night, long after the sun had set, and the plants had stopped giving out their oxygen, the lights were on in the *Halley*. Fred was leaning over the ship's work bench while Moofa and Flyball lay on his hammock, watching him work. He adjusted springs and tightened wires to rig Moofa's hammock up next to Flyball's.

Moofa knew that Flyball had told her the truth when he said that on Earth, cats kept human beings to work for them, even though she could not yet imagine the world where this was so.

At last the job was done and the hammock slung. Moofa settled down in it. As she told Flyball, she had never in all her life known such a comfortable bed, nor had she ever eaten so richly.

Fred turned out the lights. Flyball fell asleep to dream that he and his new companion were jaunting all over space on a huge mushroom. Moofa licked her whiskers as she dreamed of sardines, chicken and all the other delicacies of which Flyball had told her. Fred, it is sad to say, dreamed of chipping away immense quantities of blue glass which gathered on the tubes quicker than he could knock it off.

With the return of the sun, Fred went on with his job, glad to find that the glass had *not* grown back during the night. He was now at work on the last tube.

When the last blue shard tumbled to the ground, he straightened up.

"That's that," he said, unzipping his coveralls. "We should make a start before long. But I'd like to take a few photographs first."

Among the many pictures which he took was a colored one of Flyball and Moofa sitting on top of one of the giant lemon-yellow mushrooms.

Once Fred had finished, they all went into the *Halley*. From the door of the airlock Moofa took a long last look at the world where she had been born and which she was about to leave. Flyball gave her a friendly pat.

"So long as you're around with a space cat," he told her, with just a suggestion of pride in his voice, "you can bet you'll be back."

Fred, all his calculations made, strapped them in their hammocks.

"You'll feel awfully squashed for a moment, Moofa," the experienced Flyball told her. "But it won't last for long."

Finally, strapped in himself, Fred pressed the firing buttons. This time everything worked perfectly. There was an increasing roar and then the

Halley rose from the ground, slowly at first but gathering speed rapidly, until they felt that the springs in their hammocks could not take any more strain. After a long time of this, Fred cut the power. They were in space once more, and this time they were headed for the Moon and a well-deserved leave on Earth.

Before showing Moofa how to use magnetic sandals, Flyball introduced her to the delights of free-fall.

The red and the grey tumbled round the cabin, as happy as kittens.

01380